The Angel Babies IX

ETHEREALEMPIRICAL

Clive Alando Taylor

authorHOUSE®

AuthorHouse™ UK
1663 Liberty Drive
Bloomington, IN 47403 USA
www.authorhouse.co.uk
Phone: 0800.197.4150

Published by AuthorHouse 09/19/2016

ISBN: 978-1-5246-6324-7 (sc)
ISBN: 978-1-5246-6323-0 (e)

Angelus Domini .IX

INSPIRIT* ASPIRE* ESPRIT* INSPIRE*

Because of the things that have first become proclaimed within the spirit, and then translated in the soul, in order for the body to then become alive and responsive or to aspire, or to be inspired, if only then for the body to become a vessel, or a catalyst, or indeed an instrument of will, with which first the living spirit that gave life to it, along with the merits and the meaning of life, and the instruction and the interpretation of life, is simply to understand that the relationship between the spirit and the soul, are also the one living embodiment with which all things are one, and become connected and interwoven by creating, or causing what we can come to call, or refer to as the essence, or the cradle, or the fabric of life, which is in itself part physical and part spirit.

And so it is, that we are all brought in being, along with this primordial and spiritual birth, and along with this the presence or the origins of the spirit, which is also the fabric and the nurturer of the soul with which the body can be formed, albeit that by human standards, this act of nature however natural, can now take place through the act of procreation or consummation, and so it is with regard to this living spirit that we are also upon our natural and physical birth, given a name and a number, inasmuch that we represent, or become identified by a color, or upon our created formation and distinction of identity, we become recognized by our individuality.

But concerning the Angels, it has always been of an interest to me how their very conception, or existence, or origin from nature and imagination, could have become formed and brought into being, as overtime I have heard several stories of how with the event of the first creation of man, that upon this event, that all the Angels were made to accept and to serve in God's creation of man, and that man was permitted to give command to these Angels in the event of his life, and the trials of his life which were to be mastered, but within this godly decree and narrative, we also see that there was all but one Angel that either disagreed or disapproved with, not only the creation of man, but also with the formation of this covenant between God and man, and that all but one Angel was Satan, who was somewhat displeased with God's creation of man, and in by doing so would not succumb or show respect or demonstrate servility or humility toward man or mankind.

As overtime it was also revealed to me, that with the creation of the Angels, that it was also much to their advantage as it was to ours, for the Angels themselves to adhere to this role and to serve in the best interest of man's endeavors upon the face of the earth, as long as man himself could demonstrate and become of a will and a nature to practice his faith with a spirit, and a soul, and a body that would become attuned to a godly or godlike nature, and in by doing so, and in by believing so, that all of his needs would be met with accordingly.

And so this perspective brings me to question my own faith and ideas about the concept and the ideology of Angels, insomuch so that I needed to address and to explore my own minds revelation, and to investigate that which I was told or at least that which I thought I knew concerning the Angels along with the juxtaposition that if Satan along with those Angels opposed to serving God's creation of man, and of those that did indeed seek to serve and to favor God's creation and to meet with the merits, and the dreams, and the aspirations of man, that could indeed cause us all to be at the mercy and the subjection of an externally influential and internal spiritual struggle or spiritual warfare, not only with ourselves, but also with our primordial and spiritual identity.

And also because of our own conceptual reasoning and comprehension beyond this event, is that we almost find ourselves astonished into believing that this idea of rights over our mortal souls or being, must have begun or started long ago, or at least long before any of us were even souls inhabiting our physical bodies here as a living presence upon the face of the earth, and such is this constructed dilemma behind our beliefs or identities, or the fact that the names, or the numbers that we have all been given, or that have at least become assigned to us, is simply because of the fact that we have all been born into the physical world.

As even I in my attempts, to try to come to terms with the very idea of how nature and creation could allow so many of us to question this reason of totality, if only for me to present to you the story of the Angel Babies, if only to understand, or to restore if your faith along with mine, back into the realms of mankind and humanity, as I have also come to reflect in my own approach and understanding of this narrative between God and Satan and the Angels, that also in recognizing that they all have the power to influence and to subject us to, as well as to direct mankind and humanity, either to our best or worst possibilities, if only then to challenge our primordial spiritual origin within the confines of our own lifestyles, and practices and beliefs, as if in our own efforts and practices that we are all each and every one of us, in subjection or at least examples and products of both good and bad influences.

Which is also why that in our spiritual nature, that we often call out to these heavenly and external Angelic forces to approach us, and to heal us, and to bless us spiritually, which is, or has to be made to become a necessity, especially when there is a humane need for us to call out for the assistance, and the welfare, and the benefit of our own souls, and our own bodies to be aided or administered too, or indeed for the proper gifts to be bestowed upon us, to empower us in such a way, that we can receive guidance and make affirmations through the proper will and conduct of a satisfactory lesson learnt albeit through this practical application and understanding, if only to attain spiritual and fruitful lives.

As it is simply by recognizing that we are, or at some point or another in our lives, have always somewhat been open, or subject to the interpretations of spiritual warfare by reason of definition, in that Satan's interpretation of creation is something somewhat of contempt, in that God should do away with, or even destroy creation, but as much as Satan can only prove to tempt, or to provoke God into this reckoning, it is only simply by inadvertently influencing the concepts, or the ideologies of man, that of which whom God has also created to be creators, that man through his trials of life could also be deemed to be seen in Satan's view, that somehow God had failed in this act of creation, and that Satan who is also just an Angel, could somehow convince God of ending creation, as Satan himself cannot, nor does not possess the power to stop or to end creation, which of course is only in the hands of the creator.

And so this brings me back to the Angels, and of those that are in favor of either serving, or saving mankind from his own end and destruction, albeit that we are caught up in a primordial spiritual fight, that we are all engaged in, or by reason of definition born into, and so it is only by our choices that we ultimately pay for our sacrifice, or believe in our rights to life, inasmuch that we are all lifted up to our greatest effort or design, if we can learn to demonstrate and to accept our humanity in a way that regards and reflects our greater desire or need, to be something more than what we choose to believe is only in the hands of God the creator or indeed a spirit in the sky.

~*~

It was very much my intention not to state the name of any particular place in the script as I thought that the telling of the story of the Angel Babies is in itself about believing in who you are, and also about facing up to your fears. The Angel Babies is also set loosely in accordance with the foretelling of the Bibles Revelations.

I thought it would be best to take this approach, as the writing of the script is also about the Who, What, Where, When, How and Why scenario that we all often deal with in our ongoing existence. It would also not be fair to myself or to anyone else who has read the Angel Babies to not acknowledge this line of questioning, for instance, who are we? What are we doing here? Where did we come from? And when will our true purpose be known? And how do we fulfil our true potential to better ourselves and others, the point of which are the statements that I am also making in the Angel Babies and about Angels in particular,

Is that if we reach far into our minds we still wonder where did the Angels come from and what is their place in this world.

I know sometimes that we all wish and pray for the miracle of life to reveal itself but the answer to this mystery truly lives within us and around us, I only hope that you will find the Angel Babies an interesting narrative and exciting story as I have had in bringing it to life, after all there could be an Angel Baby being born right now.

~*~

After these things I looked and behold a door standing open in Heaven and the first voice which I heard was like a (Trumpet!) speaking with me saying come up here and I will show you things which must take place after this.

Immediately I was in the spirit and behold a throne set in Heaven and one sat on the throne and he who sat there was like a Jasper and a Sardius Stone in appearance, And there was a Rainbow around, In appearance like an Emerald.

Time is neither here or there, it is a time in between time as it is the beginning and yet the end of time. This is a story of the Alpha and the Omega, the first and the last and yet as we enter into this revelation, we begin to witness the birth of the Angel Babies a time of heavenly conception when dying Angels gave birth to Angelic children who were born to represent the order of the new world. The names of these Angel Babies remained unknown but they carried the Seal of their fathers written on their foreheads, and in all it totalled one hundred and forty four thousand Angels and this is the story of one of them.

ETHEREAL EMPIRICAL. IX

Of all the winged creatures and also of those Angels that we did not know, would soon be sent out in the many places of the world to defeat and to conquer the demons of old, as it was also said and told, that some of them had since before my duly elected and prime position, had defied God in the presences of the Angels of the Empyreans, and yet as of now they were to be set free and pardoned within this new act of accordance in that they should be summonsed to repay their debts in this service of affiliations and servitude, if only once again to become realigned in through their obedience to the will of God

As it had by now become my upmost duty and honorable position, to take after and to follow in the many ways of Pablo Establo Estebhan Augustus Diablo the Immortal one, and to begin the record the unwritten laws of Mankind's legacy unto its inevitable destiny, if not only unto the fulfillment an inconclusive and yet never ending reality, and yet even the besides the Ophanim and the throne of God, I could distinctly and almost react to feeling and hearing the penetration of a weakened and remorseful soul, each and every day, especially as the days without night was upon us, and yet still I could hear a voce whispering and crying, help me God, inside my mind, as if perpetually and repetitiously with each and every second that passed by, holding with fear and desperation, with each and every thought of expression of volatility from within the depths, set against the backdrop of an illuminous arc in the sky, along the with the narrative sound of Mankind moving and interchanging at will between infinite states, like babies unto birth becoming children and changing and growing through the passages of time, still this voice would whisper help me God, help me make it tonight.

As such was this unfamiliar soul upon souls, and yet seemingly so, to be tied to my own existential disposition and deductive reasoning, seem to relate to me in as many and measureable infinite ways, as with each and every moment, it was as though the ethereal winds would start to enter within me, and yet bother me intrusively, round and about, and even beyond the constructs of the Empyreans, along with the backdrop of the stars in the sky, as with only my aspirations left to feed upon and become resourced and replenished upon these imposing and disturbing prayers besides me, help me God in my life, as even the winged creatures circling the throne of God did also seek to utter such appalling things, as if being possessed by the eternities of time, with each and every shadow, flickering like shades lights, as if somehow these reflections of Ghosts from an eventful pass, were now by now dancing in my eyes, as within infinite seconds, I would just become frozen in my state to stop and stare in gazing upon them through the lenses of space and time, to see these blackened silhouetted souls descending before me, help me God, before Mankind dies.

For those of us who would never know in becoming oblivious to the remote absences of those souls now wandering through a repetition of the past forever lost, never to understand or to be understood, that they did indeed inhabit and take to flight from the valley of the dead, I didn't know why I shed my tears beneath a violent sky, nothing but a riddle of a fabled parable, nothing but forgiveness could I offer, as I could not even now come to know them personally or affectionately, for once too often, we thought we could escape this purgatory and getaway to embrace and to released to see the Sunshine and the Son of the Son, as if we could never ever pay our debts to debtor, with all our doubts, collected from the dawn, with no foreseeable way out, we just couldn't carry on, in the valley of the dead, beneath all the precious stones, and metals and minerals, and yet we take it that even upon its harvest that even we in becoming buried amongst such riches, that even we could not even spend or unearth it for ourselves to afford enough for our freedoms, if only for us to set out forthrightly and to take out our revenge upon the keepers of our soul cages, cold and naked upon our responses, and yet never able enough to be touched by the gratitude of our own purposes, and yet still found to be dreaming and to be loved by the Father of the Son.

For as high as the sky and as deep as the sea, we have wrestled with the ideas and reckoned with the forces that have put the fear of God inside the dreams of Mankind, and yet I was not yet reconciled and besides myself, within this Angeldom, that I would not so easily be persuaded and compelled so as to be convinced, in what it was that I was to wish to believe, as if demonstrated by Mankind prostrating upon its' knees, and yet we were pronounced and told that we would become destined for Hell, amongst the lies that we would tell, if only in the persuasions and perversions of this mystery, for it was as if it were a fairytale reinacted and played out like an orchestra's symphony in the name of the world, and the earth, and the heavens and most of all God, and yet all the lives that we would have wrecked in and amongst the wishing well of prayers, Souls, Enemies, Adversaries, all these people I swear were sworn unto an oath that they could not bear to contain, and yet there were no hiding places anywhere, even as we looked back to the beginning of the beginning.

For we have been accused for far too long for the rights and of that with which we were made to carry and to tally in amongst the abuses of these old ideas set against these rights within the wrongs of new age and new ideas committed against us, as it was written and said, and the story was pronounced out of hate, and out of rage, and out of anger, and so for those of us who were to rebel, we were told, you shall regret those words and those actions, and you shall never tell of the wickednesses that has befallen Mankind across the mornings of centuries and of when the blood did start to boil, and as of when the heads did starts to swell, believe me, for I know heaven, and I was present when the Angels Fell, for they fell when we fell, as we all fell down too broken and bitter hearts, torn apart by the passages of time and existence, and yet we with which no elixir to replenish and sustain us, and with no way to repair our wings, with no way to mend or fix the broken ailments that befell upon us and our troubles, until it was said that all such beings should be sent back to be made refreshed and renewed upon the initial act of returning to the start in placing all such beings back into the hands of the maker.

Into the hands of the void, where there's a voice, and a sense of ease in the breeze, where heaven seems to rustles amongst the trees, how can we not yet hear it, when it speaks to the heart, there's a sound, all around, and its' getting very loud, louder and louder, perhaps, can you hear it, the crowd, as they're praying, get up off your knees, for there is no time for searching, walk into the ways of Humanity, and look at how love is working, what you and I now decide to be in this life is certain, and not a mystery, for it is only a self fulfilling prophecy, there's a cloud in the sky, and its' now upon its' flight, carrying the voice and the declaration of our alibi's, don't you know that when it rains, spirits are talking, there's a whisper in the air, and its coming through louder and clearer, have no fear my dear angel for it is you and yet nothing at all, there's a story in your heart, and it was written down right from the start, so play your part, and do all that you can until its' inevitable outcome, do it all until the final curtain, for there's a star in the sky, burning inside your eyes, so show some surprise, as we all arrive at the same destination.

As all good and bad things come in threes, as such is the trinity of Mankind, like good fortune and superstition and religion, I know this much is hard to understand but I also now know that dying is also part of the plan, as with every season and just like spring, we are all born with the immortality of mortality, and every year that comes, so too do we also sow and reap, as upon this harvest which has come, and so too even as I was once a demon upon a grounded wing and demoted without a soul, then so too am I now an angel resurrected and set free and renewed with an Angels Heart, now sent forth to attend to the sheaves, as I know that this is also a part of the plan, and so the path that I must take is set out before me, so there is no need to cry and weep, as every dreamer has dreamt of eternity, and every lover has felt the breath of ecstasy, from the cradle of youth to this old ages of time, and yet somehow, the thought of departing, makes me feel that love had never died.

Venus knows that we live amongst the stars, a God amongst aliens, men and angels, and the construction of Mars and Humanity, till the ends of mother earth in our voyages to another freedom, at the end of the World!, the electric arc, set adrift on an endless sea, like a titan ship now sailing across a deserted universe, drifting towards eternity, coursing through the cosmos and the stars of a galaxy, voyages to another freedom from a distant memory, tell me angel, how could mother earth survive, when humanity couldn't stop to save her life and soul, and yet now that this new beginning has come back to the end, can it be that with the whispers of a song, that the whole thing starts again.

Open up your hallowed mind, and find the angel that lives inside, that enlightened feeling of something sublime, set as a key to unlock what's real and divine, let your emotions guide your soul through the storm from within, turns your silences into screams, express the parts of your infinite being, bringing peace to love and reality's dream, open your eyes and gaze at the Sun, for the Sky is the foundations of what the visions are to become, the elements born of earth, air, fire and water, the universal truths of chaos and disorder, make and create and state all of your virtues, be simple and humble and pious and good, enjoy every day as it comes to greet you, with a power like flowers, that's always renewed, open your mouth and breathe in with ease, the knowledge of self, that flows through your being, uncover the spirit that lives in the truth, that transcending spirit of old age and youth, believe what you say and trust what you do, and follow the path that you were destined to choose for you to go with the flow of your energy field, and live in the moment until you are free.

For I was told that life is worth more than gold, though many souls were bought, and paid for and sold, you were there whispering your prayers, where I overheard through the hymns and the sermons, as you turn your head toward the sky is it tears or rain that you hope to find, the greatest kingdom, or the grandest design cannot explain, this human life, is it me, or am I the one to hold the key, the one that leads to a path called destiny, is it you my brother, that has come to find the clues, or is it I the chosen one, and the only one amongst you, is it war, or just the writing on the wall, or just a law, to which all of us are afraid but none of us shall obey, if only to help us as we fall, or is it time itself that will free us from our crimes, after living an everlasting life.

I know that this world will not come to an end, as long as the light of life is shining within like castles of sand rising up to the sky, like a fortress for Kings and Queens, Who shall see eye to eye, for now at least we must live for love, for love is like the Lighthouse that shines within the Ivory Tower, revelations, creations of Nations, like seeds of a flower, they nurture their nature, upon every hour, as long ago as when someone told a story of a Legend old, so so far away in a remote place unknown, a Mountain High, a Valley Low, when the shaken got shook, a Mystery, a Fantasy, a Courtship full of Kings and Queens, a Kingdom stood so Heavenly, upon the Shore, a Golden Sea, for Heaven made Earth to become another world for us to see, in another place for us to be.

Within this infinite circle, we are equally squared, by three infinite triangles, we are interlinked by their personalities, and we are framed by the characteristics, we are synonymous believers, unified by the agnostics, perfected by the atheists, we are the shapes that alter destiny, we enter by the way in of the infinite circles of life, we are equally squared by the dogma of statistics, we are three infinite sides of a perfected triangle that holds every hue and every contour and every shade of the particles of this universe and the beyond, we are released by the circle of life, we are freed from the dependency of the four equal corners of the earth, and we are emancipated and liberated by the prisms of the trinity of the triangle, as it is with one single reverberation of the universe that in the passing of hundreds if not a thousand years and yet with one spoken word along with the passages of time in how long it took me to get here, as this estimation was only one proclamation and of that from the start and of one beginning.

And yet within one spoken word and the end of the dream, does not the agnostic arise in me, followed by the ideology of the atheist, along with the truth of this psychology where there is no apology, is that not the end of the truth, which began light years away, except that in one aeon, that's how long it takes before heaven is declared, and thus so, the true revelation of this occasion of destinations can be witnessed and yet hardly be recognized and seen through the heart of the prism, in containing the blue print and the original forms of the heart, and the mind, and the soul, and the perfected spirit, that which physical conscientious objectors cannot comprehend, and will not willingly pursue to be achieved, if no one believes, for that is all that is required to erase the time that it will take, where the dawn of the rising of the eternal sun shining was once and always will be only a seed for the Son of the Sun must become one with the ascent of man, within the plans, that no Man can understand of whom or of what he is as the subject of this matter.

Even though you know how it all turns out for the greater good of God, and so then why wonder if you still have any doubts left to consider, even though you know how the story goes, still you are possessed as I once was, so why do you still believe that there is something more to know, when we are pacified by the aggressors and the conscientious simple objections of the agnostics and the atheists, as even you in your attempt have tried to fight against these rules of engagement and perfected solitude withstanding, in maintaining your duty and office of servitude if only to achieve the calm of a peaceful revolution or solutions, now offered up as prayers in the peacemakers hands, which are the weapons of resolutions, and so if you possessed such a destructive tool, then would not all that stood between us and the throne of God, if they we're merely but a thousand men or more, which one of us do you think would lose, and of course the question is which one of us would end up as a fool, and who made the sky, and who made the earth, and the sea and the sand, and the rocks, and the dirt, or could it be that only one single Man amongst Men doesn't know, or maybe that one single Man amongst Men does know, and that's why it is so.

For nobody knows how it started, and nobody knows how it will end, except one Man amongst many Men, and yet nobody knows if it will ever happen again, even Darwin says that we just evolved, as an organism, so simple and yet so small, and yet so significant, maybe it's true, or maybe we will never know, for what strikes the chord and makes the heart beat inside the soul, for if science says that it all began with a crash with which they come to establish it as the big bang theory and yet some would say from the stars and other distant Planets from which we came, another species perhaps, the Angels of the Empyreans Perhaps, who just remained.

Like the rising Sun, the Son arises, and do you not love it when he comes, even though he cannot really stay, like the Moon when she arises, entering into the darkest of places, even though it seems, you were gone too soon, yes the more we linger, the more we realize that perhaps we were meant to be alone, somehow standing on our own accord, no matter how the story goes, somehow Mankind is discarded, forgotten and left outside in the cold to fend for himself, much like a door, that I once walked through, across the passages of time, once before life had closed the door behind me, and death took a hold and too me too this place forever more, but you heard me my brother, and you also felt m presence, as I now draw closer to yours, like a dream that could never be redeemed, as there is a part of you that I can now never be, like the day, that came and went away, for nothing ventured and nothing gained, like a crowd of infinite souls, I became aware that I was the one who always standing out, which somehow struck me, and I knew I was cursed to be found to be going the other way, as even sometimes it feels like the whole world is talking, and then sometimes it feels like there is nothing to hear at all, is it you or is it me, are we both so curious, or just so eager to see God in his infinite glory, is it them or us, is it simply love, or are we simply caught out with the ability to take flight and to ascend and descend at will, as sometimes it feels like I can sense everything around me, and yet sometimes it feels like inside me everything is so empty, as I always knew when I had lost my timespell, that when I found you, that I would once again live out my Angelic life.

It may not be true for your heart but except for mine, but I always knew that I would be revived, even though sometimes It feels like, that within the same moment, I had stopped believing, and sometimes, it feels like, I'm always looking for a reason, but tell me Brother, after you change the world for good, how will the politics of the day that once made heads raise up and listen, and then proceed to take a walk towards a future, that they may hardly recognize, as it could be the mist in this mystery, or the realities transcending forth from out of a dream, or even perhaps the fairiest of stories without the tale, and do not forget to sigh or breathe my brother, as it could be the exhale before the inhale, or it could have truly have been anything that you would wanted it to be, and even after now that you have unified all of the people of the world, to walk into this light, then tell how will you manage to turn these streets into Gold, as the Lord knows that this story has always been told, and after you enlighten their minds why is it that Mankind does marvel at the Sunshine in the ways that we do, is he not so easily to be held captive, and why then, does everything look and seem right, is everything to be found so rosy, and is everything clean and close to Godliness, as that was for me to be the best part of this Angel Babies dream.

If we are contrary to God, then on the other hand what are you opposed too, if the shoe is on the other foot so to speak, and if we are set free from this misery, then why do we still despair, even as I speak to tell you now of the fortunes of my independence and freedoms, but still I cling and clutch at thin air to hold me tight and to steady my nerves, and then poof, with one slip of the tongue and it all disappears, gone just like that, and we are all once again thrown into the realms of chaos, upon this the last day of the last day, even as some people still wait and some people are still waiting, even as some people have strayed beyond and away from something amazing, even as some people are lost, and yet some people are still looking, even as some people have found that things are still broken, upon this, the last dream of the last dream, of the last dream, and yet we are still patiently and eagerly awaiting to hear the last words of the last word.

Like scavengers and rodents we walk amongst the dead clinging onto Vices that once kept us misled, another shock to the soul as we take our last breath, in coming face to face with the look of death, staring at us and laughing in our faces, the last Six in a world of Sevens, the last Nine, upon the wings to heaven, the last days, since the world begun, that last number, that last number One, in a world of monsters, I curse the cold, as there is always something evil, stuck within a hole, I'm only fighting demons to save my own soul, as I know the grimful reaping comes upon us like the Holy Ghost, I'm only burning ashes, up against the Sun, I'm only haunted by shadows, of the invisible ones.

And so now you show me all the lonely souls have only gathered today, in respect of the futility of changes that affect us all, all the while, while we are waiting for the dawn to fade away, the unconditional debts and promises of the psychological heart confused while all the while, the pains of growing, learning life through the chaotic order of these family ties, the fire slaughters the burning waters, as the world is falling to decay, dying bloodlines, polluted skies, the people becoming blinded their ways, peaceful orders and the breaking of borders, as if we were all too deeply concerned in becoming to cornered to run away in search of meaning, with shattered feelings, detached from reasons, we all pray, to the hierarchy of this family of crisis, where arguments and sanctions are made with holy water, as we are warned, don't play with fire, a bottle of Oil for the Anointing and were all up in flames, it's not the ending, as we are not pretending that this love that God is sending from light years away, is only but temporary gesture, to rebuild and to breakdown in tearing down the fake constructions, and to make a will, and to find a way, for this irresponsible misplaced wisdom, in this accountability of the family tree for these freedoms are now burning and yet all is yearning to send a message of insecurities across the bridges of all eternity.

Please do not resist, for all the chances that were missed, as the time upon the hourglass cannot be borrowed, as we only live in a dream of multi realities, and yet this world we believe has much more potential to be forged in the hands of the maker, and yet the elastic will snap and the bricks will break, the wider the mile upon the road that we take with the indescribable signs, you will find are great, as Mankind maps a chart to heaven, fly to your feet, for the wind is beneath you, and if you even begin to believe that it is time to go, then sit and be still as night turns to day naturally, and you'll wonder what will God say the very moment of this second that your away in your absence, as these feelings that you find are things set aside, pronounced as the gestures and tokens of the love In your life, and yet is it not so compelling, that you are the key to the door, the elevation of the floor, to fly and rise above it all without even knowing.

Is there such a love, is there such a name, is there a way for us to hold onto the flames, is there a you, is there a me, when all around us, there is nothing left to see, as the prayers that we were once submitted made my eyes begin to smile, even though they would cry, believe me I know that I have heard every single line, and so whatever the news carrier, we are all left to ponder in just making up our minds, I could be lost, or winning every single time, but is it your will, is it your way that dictates to me, that I cannot find my space, are you the reasons why I don't know what to feel, can it be trust, can it be true, is my honesty good enough for you, then verily verily I say unto you, follow your heart, follow your dreams, and then maybe they might say, that heaven's destiny is fulfilled, even if nobody cares for the feelings I express, as this resistance that I'm feeling, I now know that I cannot find a reason why the birds of a feather flock together, for the closer we become, the more we end up further away.

As for when the ones you love turn against you, and the ones you need still reject you, as of when nobody wants you, is this not Mankind's reality bound to show, and yet how can we survive through their separation, one love, one heart in segregation, two peas in a pod could never know how this spirit could be denied a soul, the positives of talking, the negatives of procrastination and hypocrisy, verily verily I say unto you, that I was waiting on a miracle to take place, but in its' place I heard a voice in the wind so loud, is it not so easy for us to become besides ourselves, when demons are breaking down your door, is it not so easy to free yourself when trying to be just like everyone else, those smiling faces who say pretty please, always brings you to your knees, honestly, believe me its' true, all the things disturbing you, the troubles that I find are found to be with Mankind, so sincerely but not nearly you, the thunder and lightning also strikes me through and through, but outside those simple words spoke the truth, that I should proclaim this world, this universe, the galaxy for God's own playground, for the reality is to challenge one's own faults and weaknesses, and to learn to become a better you and a better me.

A redeeming force unto one's own destination to love and to experience love, at whatever cost to one's own desires and motives, to dwell alone and to come together, placed upon the right designated path, I want to thank whoever and whomever you may be, in teaching me such an instrumental and invaluable lesson, as I hope that this angel is worthy of such a worthwhile pastime, be sure to be good, for in that moment that we choose to accept each other without judgments, we become naked, and we become transparent and we become see through, and yet we become natural, and we become clear, and we become pure, and we become simple, and we become free, so free yourself and become yourself.

From since the day that you were born, a power struggle, has been going on, in the fight for the soul of Mankind, and perhaps maybe one day you were told of such things, even if they were ever mentioned at all, oh my friend I tell you now, this reality is a fantasy and a myth, oh my friend I tell you this, for I am now more than a Legend could ever be, for love over hate has conquered time, and good over evil has been laid bare upon the line, the identity and the egotistical nature of all of your troubles, with heaven and earth in tow somewhere in the middle, oh my friend I tell you this, black and white, the calls for unity, the North and South Pole, the land and the Sea, the plurality of your destination can open your minds imagination.

Like a star shining in the sky, are the inspirations in your eyes, as they say that God can erase the past, like fallen winds blowing through the trees, become the echoing of memories, and then we must insist on spending some time alone, another lock, another key, the mysteries of you and me, another love, another time, I promise you, one day You shall find, like dust and dirt inside our hands, while making castles in the sand, they say that life is symmetry, as equal to these objects that our eyes can see, like clouds and storms that pass us by, disrupting all of our precious lives, they say the volatility can break any human heart that surely waits.

Twisting and turning and burning, heating up the heart of desire, moving, growing and spreading, infecting like a fever inside, a distant star, a satellite, the endless miles, of sleepless nights, the beginning of love, the end of life, I wonder how it looks through God's eyes, shaking, and breaking the broken pieces, that have shattered apart, Slipping and drifting and ripping, tearing at the strands of the heart, falling, and dripping and dropping, ticking like the hands of time, pushing and striking and crushing, everything inside the mind, how can I tell you what I believe is true, with the odds stacked up against me, when it doesn't really mean the same thing to you, and how can the dream that you took away from me, really be the way that you wanted it to be, is it the will of God, when there's nothing more to say, is it the end of the world, waiting for the break of day, and yet I cannot pretend now, for there is no reasons why, when lovers wont love you, then there's a reason to die, and yet so many people have lost the will to live.

The architects we are in each other's dreams, like partisans it seems, we are the fixtures and the themes, the subconscious thought in the uncreated world, and yet we are realities apart, as it begins with you and me, beneath the above and much higher and we can see much higher, in being mindful of the heart, for the soul is just the start, we are the distance and the hour, much before we feel the final power, for it began some place, in time and space, way back in you past, some beautiful dream that you thought would last, that took place some years ago, you always thought it would be so, come forward out of the abyss of your darkness's, if you thinks it's' you that I am addressing, come forward, if you thought it was true, come forward, for what else can you do, for then and only then you will see that there is nobody Here, who can come back for you, my brother, we can pass the blame, my friend, we can shift the shame, we just have to tell somebody else, and they will do the same, that's the way of life, like a deck of cards, we can stand in line, like dominoes, we can fall one at a time, like a game of chess we are fated by design, what more can we ever hope to find.

We are caught up within a starlit fascination, we are the stories of this creation, somewhere else perhaps it is also so amazing someone said, why are we waiting, every precious stone, every hue, every layer in season shall simply bloom, and every thousand years, Were surely due to fill the void and vacuum, behind these walls that we build and weave, heaven is born in secrecy, beneath the highs a child can hardly see, as for what kind of world we intended it to be, did you not hear the sounds beyond the partitions as you drew near to the throne of God, did not you see the miracles, are you so certain that as every portion is measured from One to Two with the weight of your hands, as I suppose you don't even know how the water makes a Rose grow' with a Thorn upon the Root, like a flower to a Bee amongst the Dew and the Sap of the taste of the honeyed leaves, just as rain water chases after streams, as a day without God is like a year without love, no Sunlight, no Moon, as also a day without you is no way to make it or to see it through, like a Spirit to a Soul, when left disposed to growing old and alone, and I wonder' if the harvest is due, like a winter brings the cold, time always catches up with you, as the words within this book, still dreaming' to be heard as the even the preacher use to say every day without scheming or blaspheming to the Lord.

Is it not strange how these ideas never change, to be found amongst those who are excommunicated from the eyes of love, since the day, the Beloved fell from fame, struck down by the hand of God, I thought I seen the Devil die tonight, crash down from heaven, for flying way too high, I thought I heard the Devil cry tonight, but nobody cares where the eagles fly, maybe it's' jaded, if we take a chance on love, still were fated, with what is wrong and what is right, as sometimes, we stray and try to hide from sight, away from the virtues and temptations of a sinful flame, as even we upon our wings, dipped in the blood of the Innocent, well who could say, if we shall ever be free from our crimes of transgressions, and who could know if the truth would let us go into a world leaving us blind.

As I dare not tell you what to dream, as I dare not suggest to you what to believe, wrapped inside these chains, who are we with the will to wonder, who is it that made this world and set himself asunder, your forefathers were freedom fighters, iconoclastic liberators, your Angeldom legacy was forged in the dreams of revolutionaries, as I dare not tell you what you should say, as I do not know who can never be separated from night and day, but if you set me free then I will follow the stars, for that is the only way that we can truly see, who we really are, don't try to hold me down, don't keep me waiting, only freedom and love is my emancipation, as we do not have any possessions, as we only posses what we have and what we need in our Hearts, for this is all that anything could be.

I thought I'd seen the beginning of the end, come unraveling like a useless spiders web, how can everything I've ever known, turn to Purple, from Red to Blue, as it seems to me now, that falling apart, only separates the head from the heart, and it seems to me now that the voice that I heard, simply predicted, everything I learnt, running away from every disaster, the inevitable, questions and answers, naturally life Is boring and slow, but we can live as if there is no tomorrow, do not wait for me, for I've already died, from a natural cause in resurrecting my life, I know that it's hard to comprehend, but one day I hope to see you again.

And yet in love, I have tried to explain, why do we always have to live it this way, with words as we often meditate with simple invocations, for each and every day, what must the task of the token be, a simple humble spirit, of magnitude and piety, will time determine all of our fate's with the gravity and the weight, in the flights that we take, why pray every day, why pray to the Sun and the Moon anyway, if a gift is to be received, then seeking to ask, to accept to believe, for the gestures of a promise will be met with upon accordance compassionately, as it seems that our hopes and dreams, would become fulfilled by the promises we keep, a lifetime is harder to define, as a simple attribute with a purpose to be kind, for us to redeem every dream, delivered from the burden of this reality, the faithful, now down on their knees, praying for acceptance, to fulfill every need, to be taught, when a thought appears, to believe your supplication that's bestowed upon your being, can simply be forgiven so easily, granted in all of your wisdom, to set your mind free.

To want or not to want, to needlessly need something, everything, specifically ending up with nothing, unspoilt, and yet uninspired, the slipper fits, the hand in glove, the dream came true, but only for the chosen and select few, sadness looms, like misty music set adrift on lonely seas, and yet upon reflection, you have harvested the waves, and overcome the obstacles in achieving the simplest of things, in becoming contented by minor advances, a milestone in the making, and so I want you to accept a gift of the present future, I wish to reveal a secret of promises to You, made by your father on your behalf, as I also want to give you what you want, for the energy is shifting and the diagnosis is change, to evolve out of the foundations of one's own creation, through the power of one's own mind, to adapt and to entertain a new horizon.

ETHEREAL EMPIRICAL

Indeed we must ask ourselves if there was a time before time and also if there was a Kingdom before this Kingdom, and also we must ask ourselves if there a World before this World, as if by some cataclysmic event, it had become erased from the records of the unwritten laws, and if so, then it is upon this reflection and intellect and deductive reasoning as to what form does it or did it take, and also in what way was it possible to become fashioned and manifest, as it is to also know what are the basis and the roots of its' foundations, and what is the role and allied significance of God within this realm as opposed to any other realm, and yet where does this realm end, and where do we begin within the countless successions of this World becoming, as if all were so seemingly seemless in its construction, then what is it that is being caused to change if we are not changing, and yet if we have not changed then what has influenced us due to such revelations, if only to believe that this occurring thought had the means to think itself into the existences of life, then is not God all the more the ignition and the properties of our being behind this thinking, as God only requires the worship, praise and adoration that is due to him, as it is only these three rewarding merits of action that we also possess upon this distinction, and yet why should we honor him in such a way in pouring out our overwhelming love of appreciation, unless we too have become presented with such magnitude.

As even when we look back to the very source and traces of our elementary beginning, if only to unlock and uncover the severity and the instrumental truth of our origins and the authenticity of who and what we are or where we came from, and yet it is simply by the perpetual forces of nature and time, that we are forever propelled and made to push beyond these boundaries in order to move forward to meet with the forthcoming events of our ascension in order to embrace the future, and yet still we are somewhat absent and less aware and even detached from all the answers that we carry along contained within the blueprinted instructions of our infinite being, albeit it said, that it also comes from the very essence of the nature of this generative source, if only for us to answer all the necessary questions that arise and give meaning to all the precious expressions of our trials in the examination of this life.

And yet who knows how the story will end, and yet who can tell us how the story began, and perhaps maybe it only started within the seeking of truth, or perhaps maybe it might have started with reaping, if not from me then perhaps from you, or perhaps maybe it started with teaching, and yet this teaching has only yielded us the faithful evidence that leaves us no proof of these fruitful clues, or perhaps maybe it started with the weapons of war, or even perhaps with the declarations of peace, or perhaps even before the laws were presented to us from such a long time ago, and yet even as Man attempts to turn back the hands of time to zero, over and over again, the generations stand in line to march through the corridors of time, but of whom amongst the future generations shall come forth as the Son of Man, and yet who amongst them is the Son of God, and yet are they not all to be seen and witnessed and presented to us as the prophets of the ages that are given over to humanity through the courses of time, and yet is not Mankind to be challenged during this ascension, and so how are we caused to make distinctions between them if all are superior, then none can be inferior but upon equal terms and also upon an equal footing, and so do they not all reflect upon, and follow the same course of determination in uncovering the mysteries of life and God and heaven.

As I believe that we are on a path of neutral self exploration and discovery, and also one of self containment so as to extinguish the hurt and the pain and even eliminate the damage caused by our predecessors from the choices of a path that has led and brought us to experience personal suffering and the frustration of disappointments, and yet in addressing these fears and reservations that we possess, I assume that they can only serve us as a sign and signal that we should recall that even in defeat, that we should not abandon God or even love for that matter in finding ourselves becoming alone and isolated, as the real balance and difficulty is finding the truth concerning this world as we become aligned to it amongst all purposes, as I now know that we have to challenge what we can, and yet we must also accept what is beyond our control, as this is only a period of reflection and so in being true to ourselves, then it is also true to say that self discipline is not so easily achieved but sometimes requires that the heart and the mind should become steady and still with the arising of the emotions that I now dedicate to you through love and patience.

As even now amongst the stars we are born to question, did Man create himself or was Man born of creation, did Man create the World or the Heavens of the Empyreans, or was the heavens born of creation, for even as God would strike to make a soul out of earth and breathe within and give it birth, then such is Man that he would also seek to carve himself out of wood and stone in acceptance of himself, and in knowing and learning that he is also fashioned out of flesh and bone, even as creation is made to stand up perfect and true, then let us seek within these comparisons that as much as I stand next to you, that we are of an equal measure, even if eternity brings every day and every night before us, still our eyes are open and blinded by these same forbidden sights, even as Man seeks to climb up on top of the vine in reaching beyond the holy mountain of water and wine, then let us present him with the stars as he goes out in seeking to search out and to discover the face of God, and let us also succeed in addressing him as love, if only to hear him then speak these words of grace, and further still, let us inquire is seeking to learn and to know and to ask love, when can I care for you and find that you care for me too, and let us also help and assist him in simply knowing and obeying this love, in that we are determined to fulfill its' ambitions and so let us be permitted to say and to ask of him also, when can I be there for you and find that your there for me too, for the stories that we write have predicted that there will come a time, when the world will recognize a witness in this age of time.

And now that we have chartered and found our way out, much beyond the miracles of this empirical questioning and the examination of answers, patient and hungry, lost and lonely and tired of proclaiming the alchemy of fire, turning blood into gold, whilst roaming amongst the spiritual, love doesn't fade away, like other truths that we've come to know, nor does it break as other things that have broken before, as cold as the rain can be, in this temple of dreams, love is simple, as something inside me comes to fulfill a natural desire, a spirit born of fire, releasing much higher, I believe it is called a destiny of which to inspire, beneath us where the clouds bow, down where the rivers flows, and all that we'll ever encompass inside of our souls, but how can the sky high above the earth belong to a flag, and yet not to the world, as a man of the cloth must also inherit his spiritual wealth in possessing the sea, the property of God however expendable and free cannot diminish, no matter the misfortunes and fate, God makes no distinctions about the integrity of this blindness, for the salt of the earth is a simple commodity.

Clive Alando Taylor

As it was said that in the last days that men shall dream dreams and have visions, do you have a vision, do you have a dream, and are they not hallucinations of illusions, and do you have faith in these things unseen, do you have fear in this mystery such as the wise men who have a fear of God, I know the Ox can plough the soil, I know the Eagle also has wings to behold, and I know that the Lion is a King of the Earth, but what becomes of man to govern this world with such dreams and visions, keeping men in bondage and as servile masters of slavedom, if you had freedom, I would gladly have followed you in your many ways, if you demonstrated commitments, then I would have reasons to give voice and expressions to your ways, and if you had belief, then I would need your blessings bestowed upon my being to know your ways, and if you had love, then I would instantly display desire towards you, but if you broke these chains of bondage, then I would be set free from the desire of passion, and my stature would be caused to breakthrough and rise much higher.

Now here comes the morning of your hereafter, filled with happiness, joy and laughter, here comes the morning love, that you've never known, here comes the light before the dawn has said, bury your dead, and be gone from all the demons that are possessed in your head, feed your soul with prayers and dreams, think of the time that has come forth before I go in departure, fro I know that you've been dreaming about this day, and in so many ways another dream wants to born unto birth to be seen, at the end of the gates of eternity, finally you will see what the morning love will commence to bring along the way, bury the dead and heal the lepers that you possess in your head, as all the images of pictures were once only dreams, dreams that we paint upon the canvass of life, as you seal your fate when destiny calls, in all the places that call out to you come before I go, for I cannot be found on a distant shore.

We are not of this world, then how could it be that it was created and make ready and prepared for us, as it is often the persistence of the voices in the wind and the sound in the trees, that we are left speechless, never to be speak or mention a solitary word within this the Sanctuary of Haven, nothing but lies I tell you within these perpetual illusions, but how can we see if this dream of the angel babies is even real, nothing but blue sky buried in misery, the dust of the earth, how can you know which of us to trust, the east winds or the west winds, how can you know which one of us to love, the white lie or the black lie, nothing but us, nothing but forgotten souls, washed up and abandoned, discarded like scattered remnants, take your alms and your aims at redemption if you must, and seek out the dreams of your salvation, your own private emotions and personal relationship with the God of Jupiter if not any other God of whom you can make your appeals and declarations of heaven too.

As some say and pronounce forth that this is the world, and yet some say this world is waiting, but for what to behold, if not the angels of the Empyreans, although some also say that we are more than angels, then are we not human, turning to stone alone and forgotten, as we dare to speak of principles, ethics, and morals of civil proportions, until my death I cannot regret that I am dying, until my crimes are made as white as snow, I am not crying, the world is revolving, evolving, as we are solving all the problems created by Mankind, the world is rotating, even evaporating, breaking as we make and manifest a way for creation, the world is resounding, pounding and grounding itself into the elements, the world is shaking, earth quaking, elevating, to make room for its' gravitational pull upon us all, the world is spinning, twisting and turning, until we have learnt and understood beyond our own comprehension, the world is beginning, breathing, like a living organism, retreating and reverberating with the echoes of life, ending in its indefensible dimension, the world is the world and nothing else.

Pray, pray for me, for what would make the dirty clean, for when do demons become angels once more, in this holy reverential mystery, as if you could hear me speak, then speak to me, whispering softly, as if I knelt beneath the altar, then make your alterations and change me as I sit or stand imperfectly, beside the bedside of my own dreaming, for what would cause this misery, save me from this insanity, if only to potentially promise me all eternity, a victory, of the unsightly unseen, unorthodox imagining, pray, pray, pray for me, when my soul is in need of healing, from the dismay of my good feelings, is it not a good occasion, for one and all, for the rest of us, are simply here for the best of us, even God, the God of all Gods, would want nothing, except the beckoning Son, who rises with the Sun of the Dawn, the first rays of light, so don't despair in your disappointments, even the seasons will tell you so, if I have to fall, I'm gonna fall down to my feet, if only to find a prayer that is so hard to reach and yet further still so hard to define, and when I rise, I shall speak my words of truth to you, but as of yet how will you respond.

All he ever wanted to do, was to save our souls, their souls, all of these bodies buried in stone, it must have happened centuries if not aeons ago, for the body is a temple, then let us deconstruct the temple in setting the souls that desire to fly free, enough, enough of the blood on the cross, enough of broken bones, enough of pieces of silver and glitters of gold, as sure as heaven knows my name, I call on you to ease the pain in bearing the burdens of shameful blame, save our souls if you must, if you will, if you shall, but for what purpose, for this is no pretence of the solemn heart, tear down the temple of the body, and give my soul a sweetened surrender, before they leave you with nothing, nothing but God.

For what is the mind of man in a race against time, to uncover the secrets of life, searching beyond the seeds of truth, to fulfill his desire without an ounce of proper proof, for what is the mind but a force, which has yielded genocides and holocausts, as two forces colliding upon a cataclysmic high, for what is the mind if not the heart set about to play a serious part, then tell this woman of mother nature Selah, that gives birth to the wisdom of the earth, what man is worth, for man and his soul was prophesied by the angels in the books of old, no matter what man knows, he was a slave to mankind, as was mankind to humanity, to serve in love's kingdom for all eternity and beyond, to see and to witness forever and a day.

From the beginning the end, the watching are waiting, from the width, the depth, the body and the vessel that travels the breadth and the time that it takes to travel the length of the secrets of life, all are revealed within this immortality inside the mind, as are the realities so equally hard to define, the beautiful lie of a cardinal sin, that unforgivable spiritual suicide, a struggle for a fantasy, for love is peace, and war is death, and so we must abandon hate and turn to dreams, and a singular soul is released when nothing is left, the rise and the fall and the call to love, and not to armies but to the arms of faith is the only inspiration, but what is love without us, for if we lose this determination upon our destination, then whoever said God is dead has never lived, break the chains, break the ordinary formation, break away, break the fortifications, break the rules of convention, break the stigmatizations, a dream is a dream, except what is real unto who is dreaming it, to find a dream surreal, where there is no one left to defend it, defeated, living for tomorrow today has already begun, forgiven for all of our sorrows, and yesterday is long gone.

As profound as it sounds, this deconstruction of the body is also the rejuvenation of the celestial stars, in order to remove the burden that you have suffered in the wilderness of the abyss, otherwise you would lose all that is the composition of your mind, as I see that sometimes you are in despair that you do not care for God, although it seems you have also been trying in your attempts to also meet with him, and to make a declaration of heaven, or perhaps you have been anticipating something more rewarding, as it is through worrying and sighing and crying, about these things that were born of heaven now thrown and cast down toward and upon the earth, but here is the power of the sun, eternally shining for he of the one whom was sent, so harness the power of the sun, hopelessly living for each and everyone, there is no innocence here except beneath the guilty innocence of fear, but also we cannot die in the sunlight, even as did the leviathan rise from out of the ashes of angel dust, we must also rise out of the depths of heaven and earth, for love for an angel is mandatory, it is unconditional, it is also glory and freedom.

Here drink now from the religions of the water, for there is a message in the soul that is responsive as it arises, as there is no place that we can hide from sight, so pay heed and stay here for a time, as it is in the air and everywhere, ass God as my witness you are forgiven one thousand times by something you do not yet know, as much as someone, a star perhaps, is living and yet beginning to die, and so how can dying be a part of the soul, well it is not, it only a piece of the temple, come rain or shine, whatever happens to me and to my kind is of my concern, wash yourself clean in the religion of the waters, now that your soul has become discovered and found again, even if you drink it you will not drown in your quench for another day, and you shall enter the eye of the storm, another year and the passion of fears will remember to forget that you were born, birth cries from the cradle to the grave, then we are born as spirits from souls, and the body is a slave and death is the master, and life is the way, with a bucket full of sorrows, and some tears for the pain, and yet happy is the moment, that takes away the pain, revealing the secrets of life and the promises, promises that even we forgave, in order to exonerate us, as faith is believing that everyone is saved no matter how incomprehensible, when the book has been read, it shall reveal that the devil is dead.

As only he that is of himself, can now know that he has become forsaken, lost in a world cold and naked, waiting and watching on time to tell its' secrets of life to the universe, and yet he that is fallen shall not breach or reach the summit, even unto the rising of this coming event, even as we find ourselves along and upon the edge of eternity, we shall be saved the by the savior of the soul, and when the heart takes the shame and the blame away from us, he shall call out our names, and whatever will follow, we shall also follow.

As there will be no more wars in heaven, and when heaven breaks then whoever comes to be delivered amongst us, shall be acquitted and punished no more, and so before you depart from this place and enter the world below in seeking out your retribution to uproot and root out evil for your own atonement, tell me this much demon upon your resurrected birth, which were you before this judgment had come to fruition in its' passing, for I have reason and purpose to believe that I know you if not by name then at least by nature.

Well listen and hear me well Haven, for I am Angel Ruen the first pronounced consummate Angelic Son of Ophlyn the Herald Angel, defeated by the Angels who observed and prevailed over the second harvest, so it is you who bears this notoriety marked out as the legendary Angel Ruen, defeated by the Angelic Stefan Stiles Son of Hark the Herald Angel, yes it is I, he that once proclaimed the future of indifference now bowed down in shame, and in loss and regret and countless sorrows, but how do you come to be freed from this abyss, I come forth as all winged creatures are called to come forth on the day of judgment, from out of bondage through the faith of Selah's sake.

Then I shall redeem you myself, as you also have a sentient brother in me and besides that you shall rediscover that you also have a sibling kindred brother in the household of Selah, but who is this, this is his name and birth cry, which is known and presented to us as Angel Nephi of the Nephilim, thusly you are redeemed, but not because of the defeat or loss or regret of the second harvest, but because of the faith of Selah, so go now Ruen son of Ophlyn, go into the world and seek them out, for they are innumerable in number, for as I sit and as I stand, even as I am the enduring sanctuary that is Haven, from even now until the ends of the universe, I am about to change the world.

Authors Notes

It is of the utmost importance that we do not destroy any persons personal faith, no matter what or how profoundly they may aspire to be inspired to believe in something quite supernaturally or unfathomable, so please consider this and find it in your heart to know that faith is in the expression of living a life of piety and filled with a magnitude of love, as some of us put our faith in people as much as each other, as much as people put their faith in God or Angels or Spirits or Science, so I only say this, that with faith, it is only an attempt and a positive attitude that we are affirmed and just, in believing that the narratives that we are all aiming to pursue and fulfill and uncover, is to be accordingly just and right and true in our pursuits in this life, as such is the faith, that I have in all of you.

The Angel Babies Story for me, was very much written and inspired by many feelings of expression, that was buried very deeply inside of me, as it was through my own exchanges, and relationships, and journeying, and upon the discovery of both negative and positive experiences, that often challenged my own beliefs, and personal expectations of what I thought or felt was my own life's purpose, and reason for being and doing, and very much what any one of us would expect to be the result, or the outcome of their own personal life choices based upon the status quo of our own design or choosing.

The story within itself, very much maintains its own conception of intercession from one person to another, as we can only contain the comprehension of the things that we most relate too, and that which most commonly resembles and reflect our own emotions and experiences, by tying in with something tangible that either connects, or resonate at will deeply within us, as many of us have the ability and intuit nature, to grasp things not merely as they are presented to us, but how things can also unfold and manifest in us, that are sometimes far beyond our everyday imaginings, and that are also equally hard to grasp and somewhat difficult to comprehend and let alone explain.

As we often learn to see such challenges and difficulties as these, especially in young minds, that react in responsive ways and are also equally gifted, or equally find it in themselves in life changing circumstances, to deal with prevailing situations, that most of us would take for granted, and would naturally see as the average norm, as we are all somewhat uniquely adjusted to deal with the same prevailing situation very differently, or even more so to uniquely perceive it in very different ways.

As for the question of how we all independently learn to communicate through these various means of creative, or artistic, or spiritual measures, is also simply a way of communicating to God as in prayer, as well as with one another, as all aspects are one of the same creation, as to whether such forms of expression can personify, or act as an intermediate medium, or channel to God, or indeed from one person to another, is again very much dependent upon the nature of its composition and expression, and the root from which it extends, and so for us to believe that our forbearers, or indeed our ancestors have the ability to intercede for us in such spiritual terms upon this our journey through life, is very much to say, that it is through their life's experiences, that we have become equipped, and given a wealth, and a portion of their life's history, with which for us to make our own individual efforts and choices, for us to be sure and certain of the way, in which we shall eventually come to be.

When we take a leap of faith, it is often into the unknown, and it is often associated with, or stems from the result of our constant fate being applied and presented to us in the context of a fear or phobia, insomuch so, that we must somehow, or at least come face to face with, or deal with, or come to terms with these matters arising, that are usually our own personal concerns, or worries, or anxieties toward a balanced or foreseeable reality, which is often beyond our immediate control, in that we are attempting to define and deal with this systematic physical, and spiritual progression, in the hope and the faith that we can resolve these personal matters, so as to allow us to put the mind and the heart at ease and to rest.

As it is often through our rationalizing, and our affirmation, and our professing or living with our beliefs, that what we often call, or come to terms with through our acceptance, is that through faith, belief and worship in God, that such personal matters, can easily be addressed, and dealt with, so as to overcome when facing such difficult and challenging obstacles, as even when in response to a negative impact that can have a harmful effect upon our physical bodies and being, we also often rely upon this same faith in the physical terms of our living and well being to guide us, and especially where we are often engaged in rationalizing with this phenomena, in the context of our faith, hope and belief, which often requires and demands us to look upon the world in a completely different way, so that we can reach far beyond the rational expectations of our own reality, and perceive to look forward into that of our metaphysical world.

As it is through this metaphysical world of all irrationality, and chaos and confusion, that a leap of faith is required to pass through and beyond the unknown context of our rational and conscious reality, and thus so as far as we can see, to understand our consciousness, as we believe it should be, in that we are contained in every aspect of our faith, hope and belief, as we are often presented with more than just a rational imagination, of what lies beyond our eventful fate or worries and concerns, and so within the mind of dreams, we are presented with a super imagination, where extraordinary things exist and take effect much beyond our physical comprehension, although very much aligned to the interconnectedness within our emotions, that brings with it a super reality, where we can accept the tangibility of these dreams upon realizing them, so as to be found and understood, as when we are found to be waking up in our day to day reality and activity, but also in choosing not to deny or extinguish these dreams as mere dreams, but to accept, and to see them, or refer to them as signs.

As of when we see such tell tale signs, or such premonitions forgoing, or foreboding us in our fate, it is very much that these signs often impact the most upon that of our conscious minds, as they are very much presented to us in an informative and abstract way, very much like a picture puzzle that we are busily attempting to piece together and work out, and very much in the way that we are attempting to put the heart and the mind at ease and to rest, so as to secure peace of mind in order to find and establish and maintain inner peace, as such signs as these, are often the ones that I am referring too, and can often and easily be presented to us in many ways, but to be sure and certain, if they are Godly or Divining messages upon intuition and translation, very much depends and largely relies upon us as individuals, as to what we are naturally engaged in and pursuing, in the same hope and light of the context, of this experience of such a Godly nature.

As such experiences are crucial and key, as to how we deal with any or all relationships, especially when we are developing a relationship within the Godly aspects of our lives, as more often than not, when we use such phrases and metaphors as, 'Going through a Door' or 'Crossing a Bridge, it is simply by saying such statements as these, or putting things in this way or context, that we decidedly know and acknowledge that a big change is about to occur, and develop or happen to us, and so we in ourselves are becoming equipped and prepared to deal with such changes, as they shall determine what shall be the eventual outcome of our fate, as there may already have been so many foretelling signs, much before the final impact or infinite sign is presented to us, insomuch so, that it may have already been subtly presented to us, much before the true perspective or picture of our reality has come to fruition and presented to us as a whole.

The whole being, is that which pieces itself together, with all the necessary facets and aspects of our Human Nature, Personality, Mannerisms and Characteristics and Traits, as all in all, it presents to us a vision, which sets us apart from one another, but also equally ties us all together in the event and act of completing our picture and journey through life, and it is through these instincts that we all naturally possess, and is all that is inextricably woven into the metaphysical fabric and the spiritual aspects of the heart and mind, and of those that are channeled along the lines of the minds meridians, and the intricate channels that give way to apprehensible intuitive mental awareness of signs and dreams, and or premonitions or visions, of how, or what we may choose to accept, or to objectively analyze, or to take note of and perceive in communication, or indeed how God may choose to communicate with or through us.

As it is in our realizing that within our personal fate and decisiveness, that we are calling upon, and facing a reality, that questions and presents itself to us all, as something that is profoundly spiritual and ambiguous, in relation to what we are all intrinsically held and bound by within our faith and beliefs, in that what we expect is about to unravel itself before us, as we begin to discover all that in which we are, as such is the expectation and the realization in our phobias and fears, that we may begin to readdress or even regress, or desist in such a course of action concerning these doubts and deliberations, so as not to offset or to promote any ideas that may bring about any personal demise, or disharmony, or disunity, that may trigger any negative aspectual forecasts or emotions within ourselves, as it is such a self fulfilling reality, that we are all in subjection too, in creating along and upon our own individual paths of merits and natural progression, that naturally such phenomena is presented and revealed to us as a whole, and is often profoundly real and yet maintains its simplicity, and is quite ordinarily so upon our realization of it, as if by mere chance that somehow deep down we already knew, that when we became aware of it, we somehow knew it to be so.

As it is these lessons in life, that are to be learnt from such self affirming challenges, so as to test our minds imagination and of course that which is at the very heart, of how we in our Human nature, can so easily push our abilities far beyond the boundaries, upon the premise of what is, or what is not possible, which brings to mind the verse and saying of the scripture and that is to say, that if anyone adds or takes away from this book, then so too shall their part be added or taken away, and yet if we continue further along this point, it also goes on to ask, who is worthy to remove this seal, so as to reveal the dream or the foreknowledge that we may all come to terms with our natural agreement and acceptance of it, as it is in knowing and accepting what shall befall us in our fate, as to what choice of action we must or can take, as such are the phobias and fears of trepidation that also gives way to the rise of hope, so that we may come face to face with destiny.

As with each new day comes a new beginning, and with each new beginning comes new hopes and new expectations, as there are also new obstacles and challenges to overcome, as such is the dawning of life, to present to us all, such necessary and redeemable qualities within the observations of our lives, for to have hope, is to look up toward the heavens, and to quietly and silently know, that within this observation, that the sky or indeed the heavens, are still upheld by the forces of nature, that govern from above albeit much to our amazement and expectations, and that life is ordinarily and justly so, as we in our appreciation cannot always see beyond that which is so perfectly bound and set in motion with us in this universe, as we simply learn to believe and accept that this is the way of our living and all things besides us, as we are within all that has become created and laid out before us.

And yet with this new day dawning, if not for us to simply wake up and to use our hopes, and our aspirations to ascend beyond the obvious point of creation, and to apply our spiritual nature and positive will of motivation toward it, and it toward us upon reflection, as in our overcoming and prevailing, within its and our own destiny and deliverance, as such is also our descent to take warmth and courage, and comfort and refuge, when we lay down to take rest and sleep beneath the Moon and the Stars above, is also to take strength and peace of mind, in the hope and the understanding that a new day beginning, and a new dawning shall be presented to us once again, as this is the way of the life that we have come to know it, within our own divine ability and acceptance of it.

As much as life is and can very much be a challenge, it also appears to state, that there is a thread of universal commonality running through the whole of creation no matter what we profess to live and abide by as human beings, as for me the basis of these requirements that extend from this commonality is food, shelter, clothing, companionship, and a sense of connection or clarity derived from self awareness, that is not to say that there is not much more for broad scope beyond this basic measure and requirement that puts us all on an equal footing with one another, no matter where we inhabit or dwell in the world.

And so what and where are we permitted upon this universal basis, to gravitate towards, or indeed to excel to, in order to fulfill our existential experiences and engage with our full potential, as many of us in our progression towards modernity, would indeed interpret this kind of idea or philosophy, depending upon which part of the world we lived in or inhabited, as being very much viewed differently realized upon that same broad basis, which also brings me to ask, and to question, and to examine this brave new world within this context, or indeed as some would profess to say or mention, within this new world order, or new world system, as there is much to address and to consider for all concerned.

For once we have evolved and grown and matured away from our basic needs and requirements, it would also appear that many of us who have indeed excelled, or concluded in the context of a post-modernistic era of environment or society, to have almost achieved something, which is of a value, or at least on a par with something that is equally attributed, to that of a spiritual level of attainment, or indeed enlightenment, but when we address the cost of such achievement, we also begin to see that we are still somewhat grounded in our best efforts by this basic requirement, which is to achieve, acquire, and survive at will, and to endure, and to live, and to abide by such new discoveries of achievements.

As even in this progress and achievement of what we would wish, or presume to call a new world, how do we fairly address or balance, or differentiate between those of us who are yet to grasp the basis of this understanding that is required for us to excel, or indeed for us to fly, or indeed to reach the highest spiritual level of attainment of understanding, of being, doing, and knowing, as in realizing that indeed not many of us could have, or would have had the opportunity, or indeed the privilege, of exercising such expressions of freedom in our new found world.

As some of us are fundamentally held by the very conventions of what is required upon this, a basic level of our independence, maintenance, and survival, to regulate and maintain the simplicity of ourselves, and yet once we have experienced and entertained this new idea inside such a concept, our first response is how should we, or what should we do in order to engage with one another, to bring about its universality as a basic principle and as a must for all concerned, and how can it be any good for us, if indeed we all profoundly have separate agendas, or different ideals, as to what should, or could take precedence over the basic and fundamental needs to live out our lives, when food, and shelter, and clothing, and companionship, and a sense of self, or a clarity of awareness is needed at the very heart of what it is, to not only be, but remain humane.

As for the background, or indeed the backdrop, and the combining and dedicated efforts, that it has taken me as a writer to come to arrive at within this story of the Angel Babies, and of course the time that it has taken for me, to construct, and to collate the necessary, and if I may say worthy and worthwhile aspects, for this particular body of work to become written and completed within the trilogy of the Angel Babies, I would very much like just like to inform the readership, that upon exploration and construction of this body of work, that I myself as a person, have experienced several variables of conversions upon my spiritual and emotional being, upon the instruction and initiation of bringing the series of these books into the light.

For had I not been introduced into the many schools of thought and allied faiths of Christianity, Islam, Hare Krsna, Hindu, Buddhism, Dao and Shinto, that it may never have transpired or surmounted, or indeed would have been very much an arduous and challenging task, to find the right motivation for the narrative, very much needed and applied, with which to find and devise the relative inspiration, and ideas explored and written within the context and narrative of the characters and the storyline that I have presented to you as an author.

~ Clive Alando Taylor

~*~

~*~